# If We Were To Plant A Tree

Written by
## Dar
Illustrated by
## The Fourth Graders at The Environmental Charter School

Tree Pittsburgh
Pittsburgh, Pennsylvania

Hello Friends,

When my book, *If I Were A Tree*, was published in 2008, I could not have realized the amazing trajectory my career in the arts would take and how that little book full of trees would change my life. Since then, I have had the pleasure and honor to collaborate with schools, gardens, educators and organizations all over the country in an effort to connect people, particularly children, with the natural world through literacy and the arts.

I was elated that Tree Pittsburgh approached me to help them create a book that acknowledges and celebrates urban forestry. Tree Pittsburgh is a Pittsburgh-based non-profit whose mission is to protect and restore the city's urban forest through tree planting and care, education and advocacy.

Like me, the people at Tree Pittsburgh realize the necessity of trees in our world for their beauty, for their environmental benefits and for the way they mark time and place in the lives of human beings in all corners of our planet. Trees that grow in cities

Published by Tree Pittsburgh
5427 Penn Avenue, Pittsburgh, PA 15206
www.treepittsburgh.org

Project Direction and Book Design by Dar
www.darsworld.com

help us remember that our eyes adore the many glorious shades of green, that the wind loves to blow through the leaves and that the birds long to sing their song from the branches. Trees make our cities healthier, happier places to live.

This book was illustrated by a group of fourth graders from Pittsburgh's Environmental Charter School. We used found, recycled and upcycled materials to create colorful collages.

Special thanks to the Environmental Charter School at Frick and the many donors who made this book possible. Also, thank you to all the volunteers who help plant trees in Pittsburgh and cities across the nation.

A personal thank you goes to Tree Pittsburgh for bringing me into such a great bunch of people doing such cool things in this city.  ~Dar

To help in the reduction of greenhouse gases, and contribute to the environmental effort to save millions of trees and billions of gallons of water, this book was printed on recycled paper certified by the Forest Stewardship Council.

With respect and support for America, this book was printed at Bookmasters in Ashland, Ohio, USA.

The illustrations were created with collages made from "beautiful garbage." The type is Century Gothic.

Printed in the United States of America

Other Books by Dar (Hosta)

*A Walk In The Garden*
*Animalization*
*Doggie Do!*
*If I Were A Tree*
*Mavis & Her Marvelous Mooncakes*
*I Love The Alphabet*
*I Love The Night*

www.darsworld.com

This book is dedicated to the many people
who grow, tend, watch and love trees.
~Tree Pittsburgh

In memory of my Dad,
an artist and lover of trees.
~Dar

Oh, how would it be...

if we were to plant...

...a tree?

There are tree places in faraway forests and tree places in wandering woods.

There are tree places in meandering meadows and tree places in vast valleys.

But here in our working, walking,
teaching, talking, learning, loving
city we, too, need *trees!*

How would it be if
we were to plant a tree?
Here, in *this* place. Today!

What could be, for **you** and for
**me**, if we were to plant a **tree?**

It all begins
in the *smallest*
of places...

...a SEED...

A promise
of something
yet to **be**.

CITY PARK

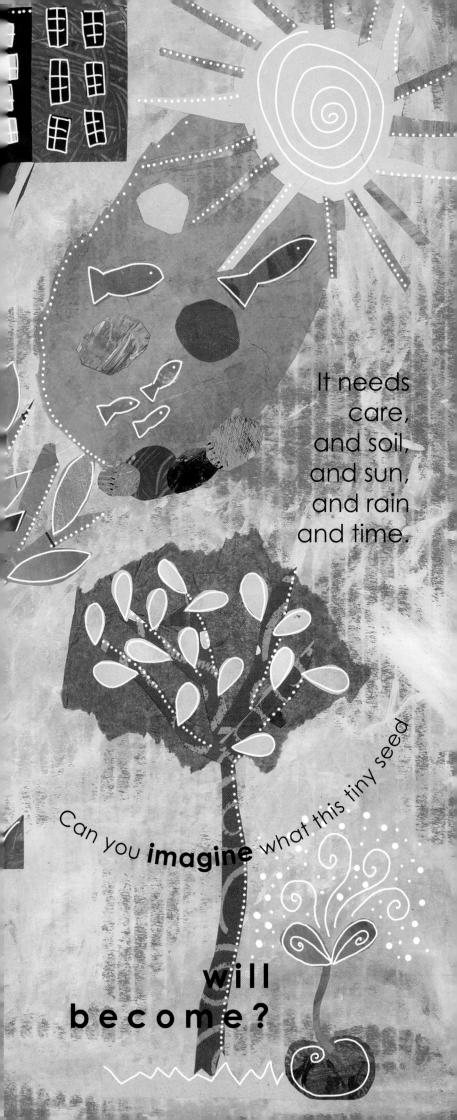

It needs
care,
and soil,
and sun,
and rain
and time.

Can you **imagine** what this tiny seed

will
become?

A tree on a busy street,
a tree in a lively park,
a tree by a beautiful river,
a tree on a playground
full of happy children,
a tree in our neighborhood
that tells us...
we
are
HOME.

Tree Helping CO-OP

Trees that keep track of **time**

and
watch
over
us
and
our
lives.

At reinvented places, small, delicate saplings grow stronger day by day.

*We tend to them so they **THRIVE!***

**SOON**

they will make

tree places,

right here...

...in our city.

Inside we **read**, and **sing**, and **learn** and **grow**.

Through the windows we see the birds **fly** from treetop to treetop.

We watch the squirrels **scamper** from limb to limb.

Outside we pretend we are queens and kings...

...living in giant castles.
We play hide and seek and tag.
**We lie on our backs**
until we are dizzy
**from looking up at the sky**
through the branches
**that stir in the breeze.**

Balls bounce and bats swing

We run fast and hard beneath a hot, summer sun.

Umbrellas of **cool**, green leaves

make **shade** for us

on the steamy pavement

where we go to catch our breath.

Trees stand **TALL**
in front of
our homes.

They make
*pretty tunnels*
over the roads

that take us from
one place...

...to
another.

We watch the seasons

as they change

and change

and change.

In the center of town, neighbors become **friends** when we work together to make gardens full of flowers, fruits, vegetables and herbs.

These are **good places**
for picnics, for conversations, for
laughter and for sharing our dreams.
These are the places that make our
neighborhood come **together**.

DOWNTOWN...

bUsY sHoPs sHuFfLe,

offices hummmmm!

Restaurants and cafés

CLATTER

The streets are LOUD
and ALIVE!

But above all the bustle

The wind makes a rustle

Which softens the sounds of the city.

Aaaaaaaaaaaaaaaaaahh!!

And, here is a place to **celebrate** and a place to **remember**.

A place for our hearts to stand
when memories bring
joy and sorrow.

A place where
**love and friendship**
live on and on.

As we look down from the very top,

from the very edge of our city,

a beautiful

ocean of leaves

rolls below.

Here, in this place,
we are all connected
by roads
and by rivers,
by bridges
and by buildings,

by parks, people,

traffic and trees.

Beautiful

city

trees!

See this small seedling?

It is full of the **future**,
ready to **grow**
and make
its **place**.

It needs **you**.

And, now, it is yours.

Yes!
**You** are a maker
of **tree places!**

What **place**

will **you** help make

by planting it

in the waiting earth?

So, how would it be?

If **we** were
to plant
a **tree**?

Not in faraway forests or
in wandering woods.
Not in meandering
meadows
or vast valleys.

But, **here!**

**In**
**our**
**city!**

HOSPITA

*Imagine what goodness could be*

*If we were to* **plant a tree!**

# How To Plant A Tree!

1. Identify the trunk flare where the tree expands at the base and remove excess soil if necessary.

2. Dig a shallow hole 2 to 3 times wider than the root ball.

3. Remove the containers or cut away the basket.

4. Place the tree at the proper height, just at the trunk flare.

5. Straighten the tree before filling.

*When we plant a tree, we help to make our communities a great place to be.*

6. Fill hole gently but firmly to avoid air pockets. Water while filling, but don't fertilize.

7. Stake the tree to help it establish itself.

8. Mulch the base with 2-4 inches of organic matter.

9. Provide follow-up care. Keep the soil moist during hot or windy weather.

10. Love your TREE (super duper important)!